Disney
Tangled
The
Series

Mixed-Up Moods

adapted by Suzanne Francis

Disk
3

studio fun
INTERNATIONAL

King Frederic had a plan. The Griffin of Pittsford was coming to visit and the king would offer him a trade deal. Though Corona would lose money, the king believed it was the right thing to do because it would mean peace for the seven kingdoms.

The Griffin was known to be difficult and the king wanted to win him over. He put Rapunzel and her friends in charge of a spectacular welcome banquet.

Inside the Great Hall, Rapunzel rehearsed her welcome speech as Cassandra sharpened an axe. "There is nothing my station isn't going to be ready for," said Cassandra, tossing the axe on top of a pile of axes.

Eugene arrived with something on wheels as he sang, "FOG MACHINE, BABY!"

Cassandra said that the fog would make it impossible for her to do her job, and the friends began to argue.

Cassandra eyed the gift baskets Rapunzel had made. "Did you really have to paint a portrait for every guest?" she asked.

Rapunzel frowned. "Do you really need six guards at your checkpoint?" She quickly apologized and Cassandra made fun of her for always being so nice.

Max and Pascal stood watching, their eyes bouncing as they followed each insult.

Disk 3
Play Tune
11

When Eugene and Cassandra started yelling at each other, Rapunzel stepped in to stop the fight. "We've all been under a lot of pressure getting ready for this banquet," she said. "How about we take a breather and go to the marketplace together?"

Even though they were still annoyed, they agreed. The friends headed out of the castle toward town.

Eugene picked up a confetti cannon.

"Put it down, Eugene," barked Cassandra.

The arguing began again!

Max and Pascal watched from Xavier's shop. Xavier explained that over time friends accept each other's flaws. He offered a mood tonic to speed the process along. "One drop for each of them is all it will take," Xavier said, handing them a small bottle.

Once back at the castle, Pascal and Max headed to the kitchen. They carefully put three drops of the tonic into some lemonade, but then accidentally spilled the whole bottle in! They watched as the friends each drank a glass . . .

Suddenly, Cassandra and Eugene were kind to each other! Max and Pascal smiled. But when Rapunzel rudely ordered them to make her a sandwich, they wondered what they had done.

Play Tune
12

The friends continued to act strangely. Rapunzel rehearsed her new welcome speech and it sounded very mean. "In conclusion, Griffin . . . Pittsford is the pits," she said.

Cassandra clapped and squealed, "Wow, that was super!" She asked Eugene what he thought.

"Me?" he asked nervously. He carefully suggested that Rapunzel say the complete opposite of what she had prepared.

When Rapunzel called one of the guards a "pinhead," she realized something. "It's like we're the total opposite of who we are normally," she said.

"I have been feeling a little peppy!" agreed Cassandra.

"And I haven't been my normal confident self," said Eugene. "And I'm really sorry for that," he said, near tears.

As Max and Pascal backed out of the room, Rapunzel called to them, demanding an explanation.

Moments later, the group stood before Xavier. "The tonic brings out the opposite of your defining personal characteristics," he explained.

When he heard they had used the entire bottle he told them it would take days to wear off.

"The banquet is tonight!" Rapunzel groaned.

Xavier told them that he could make a counter-elixir, but he would need an extremely rare three-leaved plant that grew on top of Mount Saison.

Rapunzel ordered Max and Pascal to go find the plant. The friends took the two-hour journey up Mount Saison. Their eyes popped wide open when they got to the very top—there were fields and fields of two-leaved plants to sift through! After hours of searching, they finally found the three-leafed plant and headed back to Xavier's.

Back at the castle, Cassandra was preparing for her job as security guard. "Be tough," she said, cheering herself on.

When a large ruffian showed up at the gate, he told Cassandra he lost his invitation. "Ohhh, you look trustworthy," she said and let him right through!

The Captain of the Guard scolded her. "You are relieved of your security duty," he said.

"Oh, fiddlesticks," said Cassandra.

The king, queen, and Rapunzel greeted the Griffin as he stepped out of his carriage. The king smiled and welcomed him, but the Griffin immediately started yelling.

Rapunzel glared at the short man and said, "Whoa. Insecure much, half-pint?"

The king and queen were shocked and immediately apologized as the Griffin's face turned a fiery red. Things were not off to a very good start.

Play Tune
13

Later that evening, Eugene wheeled his fog machine into the Great Hall. "Uhhhh, ladies and gentlemen, let's get this peace . . . party . . . started," he said nervously. His confetti cannon went off, sending bits of confetti all over the Griffin!

Rapunzel announced she was tired of the banquet. Then she faced the Griffin and yelled, "Why don't you just suck up your pride and accept Corona's help?!"

He looked like he might burst from anger!

Before the Griffin could get any words out, Max and Pascal appeared with the counter-elixir. It spilled into the fog machine and sprayed all over the Great Hall!

"I think I feel normal again," said Rapunzel.

"And so do I," said Eugene.

Cassandra marched over to them. "No one cares how you feel," she said.

They were thrilled to feel like themselves again!

Rapunzel smiled as she addressed everyone in the Hall. "Have I got a funny story . . ." she said.

"Boooooo!" shouted the queen.

Surprised, Rapunzel looked around and noticed something. "Oh no," she said. "The vapor reversed everyone's personalities."

The king told the Griffin his offer was a mistake and pulled out his sword. "So it comes to this," he said. "WAR!"

Play Tune
14

Rapunzel ran toward her father, "Dad, please!" she exclaimed. "You're not thinking clearly! This is a huge mistake."

The king told his guards to seize Rapunzel and her friends!

In the dungeon, they talked about their behavior. Rapunzel reminded them that even though they argued from time to time, they were still best friends and she wouldn't trade them for the world.

Rapunzel also reminded them that they never give up. "And we have a war to stop," she added.

Eugene opened the cell door with a key and announced, "Nabbed it while getting arrested."

They ran up to the Hall and found complete chaos. Rapunzel had a plan. She told Eugene to get the crowd to safety and asked Cassandra to clear a path. She would handle her father.

Cassandra and Eugene did their parts and Rapunzel picked up a sword. She faced her father and stood strong.

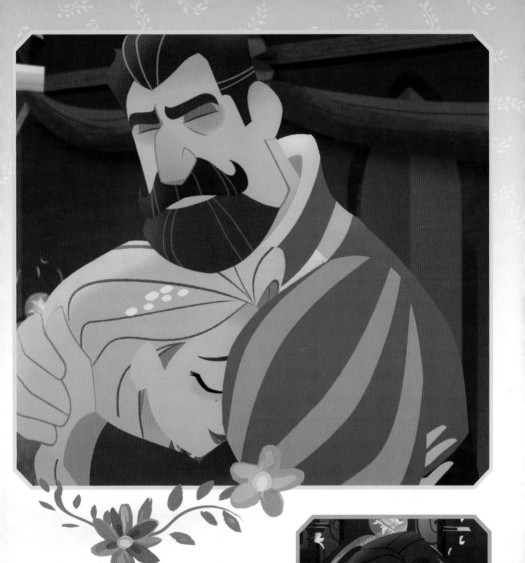

Looking into Rapunzel's eyes,
the king realized he was not
himself. The king apologized and
dropped his sword.

"Ah, come on!" said the
queen. "I wanna see a brawl!"

The next morning, it was time for the Griffin to leave. "I'm still not sure what happened last night," said the Griffin. "But Rapunzel was right. I needed to swallow my pride and accept help." He thanked her and took off in his tiny ship.

The friends were happy that things were normal again. Rapunzel took what was left of the elixir and threw it into the river, hoping never to see it again!

Play Tune
15